STICKNEY-FOREST VIEW LIBRARY DISTRICT

3 1803 00180 8989

P9-CFT-027

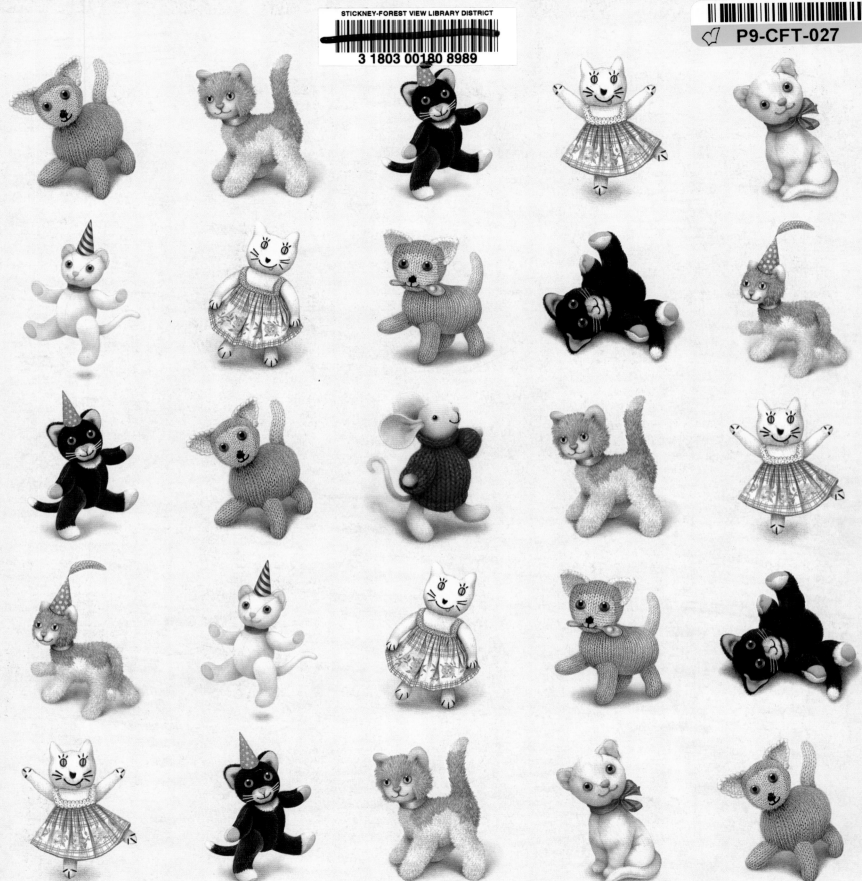

# For Matilda

## SALARIYA

www.salariya.com

This edition published in Great Britain in MMXV
by Scribblers, a division of Book House, an imprint of
The Salariya Book Company Ltd
25 Marlborough Place,
Brighton BN1 1UB

www.scribblersbooks.com
www.janehissey.co.uk

© The Salariya Book Company Ltd MMXV
Text and illustrations © Jane Hissey MMXV

All rights reserved. No part of this publication may be reproduced, stored
in or introduced into a retrieval system or transmitted in any form, or by
any means (electronic, mechanical, photocopying, recording or otherwise)
without the written permission of the publisher. Any person who does any
unauthorised act in relation to this publication may be liable to criminal
prosecution and civil claims for damages.

HB ISBN-13: 978-1-909645-96-7

1 3 5 7 9 8 6 4 2

A CIP catalogue record for this book is
available from the British Library.

Printed and bound in China

Printed on paper from sustainable sources

This book is sold subject to the conditions that it shall not,
by way of trade or otherwise, be lent, resold, hired out, or otherwise circulated
without the publisher's prior consent in any form or binding or cover other
than that in which it is published and without similar condition being
imposed on the subsequent purchaser.

# Ruby and the Naughty Cats

Jane Hissey

Ruby, Blanket and Blue were having a race.
'It's fun going fast with the wind in my face.
Look, I'm winning!' cried Ruby, but she didn't see
The Naughty Cats standing where they shouldn't be!

Why did the Naughty Cats do that?
They made poor Ruby lose her hat.

'You're always getting in the way,'
Said Ruby. 'Go away and play!'

'We're all muddy,' said Blue. 'Our clothes need a scrub.'
So they gave them a rub in a bubbly tub.
'Let's hang them to dry in the sun,' Blanket said.
'We'll just have to play in pyjamas instead.'

They'd not been gone for very long.
What have those Naughty Cats got on?

'Please give us back our clothes,' said Blue.
'They really don't look good on you.'

'I think it's time for a picnic,' said Blanket.
Ruby mixed up lemonade and they drank it.
But, while they were eating, the Naughty Cats came
And they soon turned the picnic into a game.

'Oh no!' cried Blue, 'Those cats are bad.
They've eaten all the food we had.'

'They're standing on the lovely cake
That Blanket took so long to make.'

'Let's go in my playhouse,' said Ruby, 'and hide!
If we're quiet, the Naughty Cats won't look inside.
We'll pull all the curtains and close all the doors,
Then we can do painting away from their paws.'

But, oh dear! Who's been painting too?
Those Naughty Cats love red and blue

And pink and green and brown and white.
Poor Ruby's house is such a sight!

'Let's plant some seeds that will grow into flowers,'
Said Blue, 'and these labels will show that they're ours.'
But the Naughty Cats thought they'd do gardening too,
And they weren't as careful at planting as Blue!

Look at those very Naughty Cats!
They're wearing flowerpots as hats,

And all the seeds are on the floor.

Now Blue will have to plant some more.

'I do think,' said Blanket, 'it might be less fuss
If we just let the Naughty Cats join in with us.
Let's all have a party with dancing and hats,
And if they're invited they might be Good Cats.'

It worked! The cats were at their best.
They joined in things with all the rest.

They didn't stick their paws in pies
Or play games just to win a prize.

After the party Blue Rabbit built towers.
They wobbled a bit but they stayed up for hours.
And Blanket read all of his books in one go,
While Ruby arranged tiny things in a row.

Do you know how they did all that
Without a visit from a cat?

They didn't hear a single peep...

Those Naughty Cats were FAST ASLEEP!